手斧男孩 英語求生100天
生存遊戲

遊戲說明

道　　具：骰子一顆。

人　　數：兩人以上，四人以下為宜。

遊戲方法：擲骰子決定前進步數，並按停留格上說明執行特殊動作（前進後退或暫停），先抵達終點者獲勝。

特殊說明：第8格是決定你是否需要留下來過冬的關鍵。抵達此格時，必須停下重新擲骰，擲出單數者需進入繞道過冬；擲出雙數者則可直接前進第17格，繼續冒險。

成功
前進

收服臭鼬當寵物，
前進一步

寒意颯颯，
冬天即將來臨…寒意

START
陪著你的
只有手斧一把

停！你找到無線電了！
（請重新擲骰）

單數 ▶ 往第9格過冬
雙數 ▶ 往第17格冒險

找到莓果填飽肚子，
前進兩步

遭受豪豬攻擊，
暫停一次

看到飛機殘骸

成功生火！

捕得大魚，
生存機會提高！

被麋鹿撞傷
又遇上龍捲風，
後退兩步

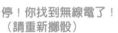

手斧男孩 之 英語求生 100天

手斧男孩中英名句選

[蓋瑞‧伯森◎著]

歷險指數＞★★★★★ **關鍵字**＞手斧男孩、領帶河、另一種結局、鹿精靈、獵殺布萊恩
挑戰關卡＞英文能力、膽大、心細 **伴讀利器**＞輕鬆的心、旺盛的求知欲、英文字典
閱前警語＞懶惰蟲、膽小鬼，切勿靠近！ **閱讀建議**＞英文其實好玩！

野人

CONTENTS

目　錄

CONTENTS

首部曲

手斧男孩
Hatchet

Hatchet

★歷險指數　↘↘↘↘↘

★關 鍵 字　墜機、大黑熊、龍捲風、活下去

★挑戰關卡　餓！餓！餓！吃！吃！吃！

★伴讀利器　手斧、勇氣、常識、電視、膽識

★閱前警語　膽小者千萬勿試！

★閱讀建議　切勿上癮，解癮祕方只在第二集《領帶河》！

生存指數測驗　　你能活著回來嗎？

年僅十三歲的你僥倖從墜機災難中生還，但是在一片叢林中，你唯一可用的工具是一把手斧。你會：

A.用手斧丟野兔來獵食　　　　　　　B.用手斧劈柴來生火

C.用手斧劈死自己　　　　　　　　　D.用手斧劈泥巴來發洩情緒

想知道解答？先跟著布萊恩冒險吧！

Hatchet

01

一切都停止了。他的內心深處，布萊恩・羅伯森內心最深處，遭到電光般的恐懼侵襲。強烈的恐懼使他的呼吸、他的思緒，甚至他的心臟都幾乎停擺。

—— 《手斧男孩》，p27

All was stopped. The very core of him, the very centre of Brian Roberson was stopped and stricken with a white-flash of horror, a terror so intense that his breathing, his thinking, and nearly his heart had stopped.

十三歲的布萊恩，暑假期間搭乘雙人小飛機要去探望在北方油田工作的父親。沒想到飛機駕駛在飛行途中突然心臟病發身亡。巨大的恐懼，讓布萊恩頓時腦海一片空白……

02

只剩他獨自一人。
在一架沒有駕駛，卻還轟隆飛行著的飛機裡，獨自一人。

—— 《手斧男孩》，p28

He was alone.
In the roaring plane with no pilot he was alone.

布萊恩置身七千呎高空的小飛機裡，他既不會開飛機，也不懂如何使用無線電求救。唯一能做的，只是盡量讓飛機減速，然後撞擊迫降……

03

運氣，他想。我運氣好，幸運之神眷顧了我。但他很清楚，事實並非如此。

——《手斧男孩》，p51

Luck, he thought. I have luck, I had good luck there. But he knew that was wrong.

即將撞毀的飛機如石塊般，落入一片湖邊空地上。布萊恩全身縮成一團，跟著飛機打滾，撞上樹林，猛烈衝進湖水裡。布萊恩費力掙脫出機身，心想，自己本來可能因為墜機而喪命，能活下來，是因為運氣好嗎？

04

布萊恩曾有位名叫裴必奇的英文老師，他總是說人要積極、要正面思考、要能掌握局面。裴老師是這麼說的：要積極，要掌控局面。

——《手斧男孩》，p59

Brian had once had an English teacher, a guy named Perpich, who was always talking about being positive, thinking positive, staying on top of things. That's how Perpich had put it —— stay positive and stay on top of things.

布萊恩清醒後，開始思考，但所有事情既混亂又沒有道理，他抑制慌亂的心情，一件件釐清。最後，布萊恩發現最大的問題是，他餓了，而且一無所有。他試著找點事來做，才不會一直想著食物，於是想起了裴必奇老師的話……

05

剎那間，他因自憐自艾而瀕臨崩潰。又髒又餓、遭叮咬、受傷；孤單、醜陋又害怕，悽慘之至，猶如身陷無底深淵，無處可逃。

——《手斧男孩》，p76

He was, at that moment, almost overcome with self-pity. He was dirty and starving and bitten and hurt and lonely and ugly and afraid and so completely miserable that it was like being in a pit, a dark, deep pit with no way out.

布萊恩找到了臨時棲身之所，也找到填飽肚子的莓果。但野外的嚴苛生活，依然在肉體與心靈上打擊著他。看見自己水中醜陋的倒影，布萊恩終於情緒崩潰……

06

他的腦子說道：那頭熊真要的話，早就吃了你。這是一件需要瞭解，而不是要逃離的事，布萊恩想著。那頭熊在吃莓果，不是吃人。

——《手斧男孩》，p80

If the bear had wanted you, his Brian said, he would have taken you. It is something to understand, he thought, not something to run away from. The bear was eating berries. Not people.

毫無野外生活知識的布萊恩，只得靠著神農嘗百草的精神尋覓食物。意外找到了成熟甜美的樹莓，卻發現有隻大黑熊也來享用這道美食。再次與死亡面對面的布萊恩，開始思考熊與人在森林裡的互動……

07

他不知道自己哭了多久。後來回顧這個在暗穴角落獨自哭泣的時刻，他認為，就是在當時學到「求生」最重要的守則，也就是自憐自艾沒有用。自憐不僅是錯事，是不該做的事，更重要的是 —— 自憐根本無濟於事。 —— 《手斧男孩》，p85

He did not know how long it took, but later he looked back on this time of crying in the corner of the dark cave and thought it as when he learned the most important rule of survival, which was that feeling sorry for yourself didn't work. It wasn't just that it was wrong to do, or that it was considered incorrect. It was more than that —— it didn't work.

布萊恩被夜裡闖入棚屋的豪豬攻擊。反擊失敗的布萊恩腳痛得要命，再次自憐自艾起來。但哭完之後，他也體認到，要活下去，就一定要拋棄這種負面情緒……

布萊恩發現，從火花到火，是一段漫長的過程。

火到底如何生成？他回想起學校，回想起所有科學課程。他是否學過如何生火？ ——《手斧男孩》，p90、93

Brian found it was a long way from sparks to fire.

What makes fire? He thought back to school. To all those science classes. Had he ever learned what made a fire?

豪豬事件不但讓布萊恩堅定信心，也想起火對人類的重要性。手斧雖然沒有打中豪豬，卻在石頭上擊出一串火花。布萊恩開始認真思考要怎麼製造出火焰……

我有朋友了，他想 —— 我現在有個朋友了。雖然是個飢渴的朋友，卻是好朋友。我有個名叫「火」的朋友。既是朋友，也是守衛，他想。

——《手斧男孩》，p94、95

I have a friend, he thought —— I have a friend now. A hungry friend, but a good one. I have a friend named fire. A friend and a guard, he thought.

布萊恩終於生起第一道火，也發現火的「食欲」遠比他預期更龐大，功能更多。他努力從森林中蒐集枯枝當作燃料，好靠火來抵擋動物和蚊蟲的侵襲。熊熊的火焰不但給了布萊恩生活的保障，也讓他開始有了存活的契機……

10

食物。

這不僅是蛋，不僅是知識，這比任何東西都重要，因為這是食物。

—— 《手斧男孩》，p100

Food.
More than eggs, more than knowledge, more than anything, this was food.

> 布萊恩沿著鱷龜的痕跡找到了鱷龜蛋。這些蛋讓布萊恩壓抑許久的飢餓感猛然爆發。他明白找到這些蛋對他的意義非比尋常……

11

現在一個聲音傳來時，他不只是聽見，還能領會那個聲音。看見東西時，無論是樹叢裡揮動翅膀的鳥，或是水面的漣漪 —— 他是真正看見那事物，而不再像在都市裡那樣只是注意到而已。現在他會看到整體。

—— 《手斧男孩》，p105

When a sound came to him now he didn't just hear it but would know the sound. And when he saw something —— a bird moving a wing inside a bush or a ripple on the water —— he would truly see that thing, not just notice it as he used to notice things in the city. He would see all parts of it.

> 在身體因為野外嚴苛生活日漸消瘦的同時，布萊恩注意到，自己的心理已經不同於以往，他對事物的看法也有了全新的觀點。

12

用他的弓，用他親手製造的箭，他取得食物，找到生存之道了。

—— 《手斧男孩》，p122

With his bow, with an arrow fashioned by his own hands he had done food, had found a way to live.

布萊恩先是做了一支魚叉，但毫不管用，魚兒總是在戳刺之前就閃開了。他決心製作一把弓。這把弓也是一場災難，差點兒就把自己的眼睛弄瞎。經過無數錯誤與挫敗之後，他終於搞懂了湖水的屈光會讓他瞄不準魚，也第一次射中了獵物。

13

這天終了，天黑之時，布萊恩躺在營火旁，帶著鼓滿魚肉的肚子和油膩膩的嘴巴，感覺到新的希望從內心深處升起。

—— 《手斧男孩》，p123

By the end of that day, when it became dark and he lay next to the fire with his stomach full of fish and grease from the meat smeared around his mouth, he could feel new hope building in him.

布萊恩的覓食能力已經從採集進步到漁獵。那一天，他給自己辦了一個吃到飽的饗宴。不停來回於湖水與火堆間，盡情地捕魚、盡情地吃。他發現自己的心態從等待救援的渴望，轉變成要靠自己堅忍求生的希望。

14

食物就是一切，就這麼簡單。森林中的萬物，從昆蟲到魚類到熊，總是永遠在尋找食物 —— 覓食，是自然界中獨尊的驅動力。吃，一切萬物都必須吃。

—— 《手斧男孩》，p124

Food was simply everything. All things in the woods, from insects to fish to bears, were always, always looking for food —— it was the great, single driving influence in nature. To eat. All must eat.

在父母庇蔭下成長的布萊恩雖然體認到食物的重要，卻忽略了食物對其他動物的強大吸引力，因而召來臭鼬的搶奪與攻擊。

15

四周有鳥，而他有眼睛 —— 他只要讓眼睛看到鳥就行了。

—— 《手斧男孩》，p133

There were birds there, and he had eyes —— he just had to bring the two things together.

布萊恩開始想要捕鳥。但即使是看起來呆頭呆腦的「傻瓜鳥」，也能夠輕易逃過他的捕殺。屢試屢敗的布萊恩這才驚覺，他獵鳥的方法是錯的……

16

他想，要有耐心。這一切大多是耐心成就的，是等待、思考，再加上用對的方法做事。這一切，還有整個生活，大多是耐心和思考的成果。

　　　　　　　　　　　　　　　　　　　　── 《手斧男孩》，p137

Patience, he thought. So much of this was patience ── waiting and thinking and doing things right. So much of all this, so much of all living was patience and thinking.

> 布萊恩終於抓到第一隻傻瓜鳥，也有了生平第一次宰殺鳥類的經驗。不過從沒下過廚的布萊恩，無法好好掌握烤鳥的火候。這時候他才發現，耐心是野外求生的一項成敗關鍵……

17

我始終感覺飢餓，不過現在能應付了，我能取得食物，知道自己有能力取得食物，這使我向上提升了。我知道我有能力。

　　　　　　　　　　　　　　　　　　　　── 《手斧男孩》，p140

I am always hungry but I can do it now, I can get food and I know I can get food and it makes me more. I know what I can do.

> 抓到傻瓜鳥之後，布萊恩終於有了羽毛可以製作更好的箭，可以更正確地飛出，這是他的「首箭日」，隨即而來的是「首兔日」── 他獵到了第一隻兔子。布萊恩跟從前再也不一樣了，他已經可以靠自己的力量獲取食物……

18

回到營地爬進棚屋後，他滿懷感激，感激炭火仍在發光；想到每天早上第一件事是把當天需要的柴火找足，他就感激每次都會找足兩、三天分的柴火；感激他需要食物時附近就有魚；最後，打著盹即將入睡之際，他感激自己還活著。　　　——《手斧男孩》，p144

When he got to the shelter he crawled inside that he had thought to get wood first thing in the mornings to be ready for the day, grateful that he had thought to get enough wood for two or three days at a time, grateful that he had fish nearby if he needed to eat, grateful, finally, as he dozed off, that he was alive.

 布萊恩被麋鹿撞傷。勉強爬回棚屋的他必須休息幾天。這時候布萊恩卻滿懷感激，感激自己已經有柴火和食物的儲備，而且感激自己沒有送掉小命⋯⋯

19

命運的銅板輕輕一擲，他就成了輸家。

不過，這次不一樣，真的不一樣了，他想，我或許遭到襲擊，但還沒倒下。

他變了，變得堅強。我在必要的時候是堅強的，我的意志堅強。

——《手斧男孩》，p147、148

A flip of some giant coin and he was the loser.

But there is a difference now, he thought —— there really is a difference. I might be hit but I'm not done.

He had changed, and he was tough. I'm tough where it counts —— tough in the head.

 禍不單行，麋鹿攻擊過後的夜晚，又有一場龍捲風來襲，瘋狂的力量不僅讓布萊恩疼痛不堪的身體再次受到傷害，也毀了他的家園和工具。但從裡到外已煥然一新的布萊恩，不再輕易就被擊倒，他決心靠自己和手斧，重建家園……

20

他不知道自己究竟能不能離開這裡，現在仍無從知曉答案，不過最後若回到家，回到從前的生活方式，情況會不會剛好相反？

——《手斧男孩》，p157

He went to sleep thinking a kind of reverse question. He did not know if he would ever get out of this, could not see how it might be, but if he did somehow get home and go back to living the way he had lived, would it be just the opposite?

龍捲風來襲，讓布萊恩有機會回到飛機裡取得救生包。但在製造木筏向飛機殘骸前進的同時，布萊恩心裡也開始感到迷惘——如果能回到從前的生活方式，會不會反過來懷念在大自然生活的一切？

能活下來的是？……

第7頁的小測驗，可以知道你在碰上困難時的應變態度與生存指數。看看你是哪一種類型吧！

選**A**的你：魯莽型　　　　　　　　　　　　　　　生存指數 68%

你雖然很清楚自己的目的，但往往用錯方法。建議你在行動前先想一想，才不會事倍功半！

魯莽型的你能得到救生包嗎？

就算讓你順利拿到救生包，也會因為手腳粗魯而把緊急發報機弄壞……天意啊！你就翻到第40頁，準備過冬吧！

選**B**的你：冷靜型　　　　　　　　　　　　　　　生存指數 92%

凡事冷靜處理的你，總是設法突破困境。就算被丟到撒哈拉沙漠，一樣能活著回來啦！

冷靜型的你能得到救生包嗎？

取得救生包與緊急發報機後，你會經過一番研究再發出求救訊號。趕快收拾東西，準備前進第22頁的領帶河吧！

選**C**的你：絕望型   生存指數 0%

你總是太快否定自己，看不見身邊的優勢。應該要更有信心，相信自己一定能平安度過！

✈ 絕望型的你能得到救生包嗎？

既然你已經劈死了自己，當然就結束啦。建議你再從第6頁開始，學習布萊恩不屈不撓的精神吧！

選**D**的你：情緒型   生存指數 54%

情緒會讓你不但無法掌握事實，還會喪失時機。記得要隨時保留體力、維持理性！

✈ 情緒型的你能得到救生包嗎？

你可能會因為種種擔憂與恐懼而猶豫，錯過得到救生包的機會。只能翻到第40頁，努力熬過寒冬吧！

手斧男孩²

領帶河

The River

The River

- ★歷險指數　↘ ↘ ↘ ↘
- ★關　鍵　字　河流、木筏、地圖、堅持下去
- ★挑戰關卡　昏迷！擱淺！邪惡念頭！
- ★伴讀利器　邏輯、勇氣、膽識、毅力
- ★閱前驚語　缺乏自信者，切勿上船！
- ★閱讀建議　冷靜，坦然面對自己內心的邪惡吧！

01

「我們當然會做一些愚蠢的試驗，好比說到野外，假裝在求生存。但在我們的實驗裡，沒有人真的必須在危機四伏的狀態下求生，」他的雙眼直視布萊恩，「就像你那樣。」 ——《領帶河》，p17

"Oh, we do silly little tests, you know, where we go out and pretend to survive. But nobody in our field has ever had to do it ─── where everything is on the line." He looked directly at Brian. "Like your."

 重返都市的布萊恩，受邀擔任政府真正的野外求生教練⋯⋯

02

「我所說的飢餓，不是妳想的那種。不是少吃了一餐，想多吃一點，或者是一整天沒吃東西的那種飢餓。我說的是，根本不知道自己能否再吃到東西，不知道還會不會有食物。糧食斷絕。沒得吃，沒得吃，還是沒得吃；到最後，仍然沒有東西吃，就算死了、消失了，還是沒有任何食物！我所說的飢餓，是那種飢餓！」

——《領帶河》，p37

"I don't mean hunger like you're thinking of it. Not just when you miss a meal and feel like eating a little bit. Or even if you go a day without eating. I mean where you don't think you're ever going to eat again —— don't know if there will ever be more food. An end to food. Where you won't eat and you won't eat and then you still won't eat and finally you still won't eat and even when you die and are gone, even then there won't be any food. That kind of hunger"

有一天布萊恩的媽媽問他，「最糟的部分是什麼？」布萊恩的回答是「飢餓」。他已經學到，大自然的法則是，食物是活命唯一的依靠。

03

剎那間，就在同一秒鐘，他變了。徹頭徹尾改變了。突然之間，他變成之前在湖邊的那個他，變成這環境的一分子，和四周融為一體。和四周融為一體，於是，任何……一件……微不足道的……事情，此刻都變得重要。　　　　　　　　　　── 《領帶河》，p45

Then, instantly — in just that part of a second — he changed. Completely. he became, suddenly, what he'd been before at the lake. Part of it, all of it; inside all of it so that every...single...little... thing became important.

> 布萊恩答應政府的請求，和心理學家德瑞克一起前去「複習」他的經歷。一下飛機，布萊恩就像開關打開一樣，變了一個人。

04

「我們是有麻煩了。整件事就是這樣。你想要學，但如果留了後路，就不過是一場遊戲罷了，一點也不真實。」　　　　　　　── 《領帶河》，p47

"We have trouble. That's what this is all about. You want to learn, but if you have all that backup, it's just more games. It's not real."

> 布萊恩要求德瑞克遣回所有求生設備，兩人只能各留一把小刀。理由是，如果不恢復到墜機當時的條件，怎麼能夠真正學到他所學到的一切？

05

「你得靜下來，」布萊恩對他說：「心要靜。有些戰鬥你是贏不了的，我想這大概就是其中之一。情況會不斷的惡化，直到過了午夜，寒意來襲時，蚊子才會停手。」 ——《領帶河》，p56

"You must settle," Brian told him. "In your mind. There are some fights you can't win, and I think this must be one of them. It will get worse and worse until after the middle of the night, when the coolness comes and the mosquitoes will stop."

> 手邊什麼都沒有的兩個人，被蚊蟲干擾得坐立不安。但是布萊恩決定要讓德瑞克明白，大自然就是這樣，只能去配合。

06

「就像換上空包彈一樣。」他輕輕笑了，「我會在下次會議時更改這些，這是錯的，心理上的錯誤。你是對的，把東西全部留在飛機上，絕對是正確的。」 ——《領帶河》，p59

"To take the edge off." He laughed softly. "I'll change that the next time we have a meeting. It was wrong. Psychologically wrong. You were right to leave all that in the plane —— absolutely right."

> 蚊蟲慢慢退去，德瑞克親口承認既然要重演布萊恩的遭遇，就不該「準備妥當」。這短短的認同之語，後來竟成了支持兩個人的支柱。

07

「就這個意思。在野外，在大自然，在這個世界上，食物就是一切。沒有食物，其他的一切，包括人類、萬事萬物，全都沒有意義。我所做的就是這樣，不斷去想食物的事。看看其他動物，鳥、魚，甚至螞蟻，都是用全部的時間在張羅食物，找東西吃。這才是大自然的真實面貌。找吃的。當你出門在外，想要生存，就要找食物。食物優先。食物，就是食物。」

——《領帶河》，p67

"Just that. Out here, in nature, in the world, food is everything. All the other parts of what we are, what everything is, don't matter without food. That's all I did —— think of food. You watch other animals, birds, fish, even down to ants —— they spend all their time working at food. Getting something to eat. That's what nature is —— really —— getting food. And when you're out here, having to live, you look for food. Food first. Food. Food."

➤ 早上了，布萊恩得開始動手打點一切，食物、火、一個棲身之處，布萊恩一邊做事、一邊對德瑞克講解：最重要的事情，就是食物……

08

他永遠忘不了他的第一堆火，那火焰對他意義重大，就像對遠古人類的重要性一樣。現在，他幾乎把生火當成是一種宗教體驗了。

——《領帶河》，p74

He would never forget the first fire, what it had meant to him —— as important as it must have been to early man —— and he approached making a fire now almost as a religious experience.

布萊恩找到打火石後，他開始找其他生火所需的東西，得先幫火打造一個安穩舒適的床，火才會進駐，布萊恩想起了生火這件事與他的關係……

09

「沒有任何事情讓情況變得棘手，一切順遂。但在真實情況下，在我先前面臨的情境裡，所有事情都不按牌理出牌，且每況愈下！飛機並不是安全降落地把我送到岸邊，而是墜落，還死了一個人！我也受了傷！我不知所措，還差點喪命！而現在我們卻在這裡裝模作樣。我抓到一條魚嘍！這裡有好多莓果耶！」 ──《領帶河》，p82

"There's not a thing to make it rough...nothing wrong. It a real situation, like when I was here before, there were things wrong ── going wrong. The plane didn't land and set me on the shore. It crashed. A man was dead. I was hurt. I didn't know anything. Nothing at all. I was, maybe close to death and now we're out here going la-de-da, I've got a fish; la-de-da, there are some more berries."

情況順遂到布萊恩開始害怕。大自然的詭譎多變，讓布萊恩知道沒有一帆風順這回事。他們什麼困難都沒有遇上，反而讓布萊恩擔心起來……

10

他被爆炸聲驚醒。

那爆炸聲彷彿發自他的頭顱，從他的思緒、夢境而來。尖銳的爆裂聲讓他猛然驚醒，打了個滾。他站起身來，不假思索地跑到棚屋後，他甚至沒有意識到自己正在移動。　　　　——《領帶河》，p86

He was awakened by an explosion.
It seemed to come from inside his skull, inside his thinking, inside the dream: a sharp crack, so loud that he snapped awake, rolled over, and was on his feet, moving to the back of the shelter without thinking, without knowing he was moving.

布萊恩忍不住要說自己烏鴉嘴了。前不久才嫌日子好過，兩人現在卻大難臨頭。不知道是倒楣還是做了什麼壞事，兩人竟遭雷擊……

11

昏迷不醒。

現在，那個字眼浮現。他以前曾經害怕死亡這個字眼，現在則對另一個字眼感到恐懼：昏迷。不能再這樣下去，不能再像以前那樣，他必須面對現實。　　　　　　　　　　　　　—— 《領帶河》，p98

In a coma.

There. That word came. He had been afraid of the word death before and now this word, coma. He'd have to stop that, have to face things better than he was facing them.

> 被雷劈中的德瑞克昏迷不醒，唯一求救用的無線電也被雷劈壞了。布萊恩雖然好運醒了過來，但是卻面臨比上次更大的問題—— 除了自救，他還得救人！

12

如果他留在這兒，德瑞克就死定了。

如果他完成航程，帶著德瑞克順流而下，至少還有機會。

布萊恩沒有選擇餘地。　　　　　　　　　　　　　—— 《領帶河》，p116

If he stayed, Derek would die.

If he made the run, took Derek down the river, at least there was a chance.

He had no choice.

> 布萊恩找到一張地圖，上面標示只要順流而下，就有交易站可以求救。儘管製造木筏將德瑞克運下去看來非常困難，但是別無他路可走……

13

他從來不曾置身這樣的處境，他十分惶恐。雖然他曾身陷險境，雖然他曾必須為生存而奮鬥，但他的抉擇只會影響自己，不會波及別人。

　　　　　　　　　　　　　　　　　　　　——《領帶河》，p126

He had never been in this position, and it frightened him. Even when he was in danger, even when he had to fight just to live, his decisions only affected him —— never another person.

布萊恩花了很大的工夫造了一艘木筏，準備啟航，啟航前他發現自己內心的猶豫和掙扎：他的抉擇將會影響到另一個人的生命⋯⋯

14

他再次確認了德瑞克的呼吸和心跳 —— 他驚覺，他幾乎是不假思索地在做這件事。才過幾個鐘頭，不過一天半而已，他已經自動反應了。

—— 《領帶河》，p131

He checked the breathing and heartbeat again and he was surprised to see that he did it almost automatically. It had just been hours —— just over a day and a half —— and he was already reacting automatically.

啟航前一刻，布萊恩仍舊不放心，如果德瑞克有任何好轉，他會馬上取消計畫在原地等候救援。這時，他發現自己似乎開始學會怎麼照顧別人、自動自發地去查看別人的狀況。

15

啟航後的第一個晚上，布萊恩又多瞭解了自己一些。
自己並不完全是善良的。

—— 《領帶河》，p143

It the night, that first night, he learned some things about himself. Not all of them were good.

缺乏睡眠、長時間勞動、過度疲勞、幻覺侵襲……種種因素，讓布萊恩的意志力開始瓦解，他看見了自己心中的邪念……

16

要是德瑞克不在就好了，又有什麼差別呢？他蠢到站起身來被閃電擊中，他早就該消失了。

布萊恩低頭看著這個不動的身軀，想了又想，想了又想……這些念頭太可怕了，他無法相信自己竟然會這樣想，但這些念頭的確存在。

—— 《領帶河》，p149

It would be better if Derek were gone. What was the difference? He was dumb enough to rise up and get hit by the lightning, and he should be gone.

Brian looked down at the still form and thought the thought; and it was so awful that did not believe he was thinking it, but it was there, the thought.

木筏停滯不前。疲憊到臨界點的布萊恩，開始埋怨德瑞克，甚至希望快點擺脫這個累贅。這個念頭讓布萊恩自己都嚇一跳，沒想到人在面臨絕境的時候，竟然會出現這麼強烈的恨意……

17

「謝謝你。」他低語著,也意識到這似乎是另一種形式的禱告。他深深感激的不只是河水、水流、前行,對其他事,同樣滿懷謝意。和德瑞克一起熬過這個夜晚……感激自己熬過去了。

——《領帶河》,p150、151

"Thank you," he whispered, and realized when he said it that it was another kind of prayer and that he was grateful not just for the river, the current, the movement —— but the other thing as well.
Coming through the night with Derek ... grateful that he had made it.

終於,在黎明之前,布萊恩划回了河道,木筏又得以順著水流前進。布萊恩辦到了。他感謝這一切……

18

時間很詭異,它毫無意義,卻又代表一切。就像食物一樣,缺乏的時候渴望,充盈的時候又不在意。 ——《領帶河》,p155

Time was so strange. It didn't mean anything, then it meant everything. It was like food. When he didn't have it he wanted it, when there was plenty of it he didn't care about it.

木筏現在平穩地前進,早晨驅散了夜裡的疲倦和疼痛,卻也帶來了飢餓感,布萊恩強迫自己不去想食物,而是計畫自己該做什麼、計畫自己如何繼續前進。

19

他努力對抗驚慌失措的情緒。

事情就是如此。如果木筏翻了，或者德瑞克從木筏上掉下來，那麼……那麼，也就只能這樣了。

如果不是的話，德瑞克或許仍安然無恙。　　　——《領帶河》，p168

He fought panic.

Things were —— were what they were. If the raft rolled or if Derek fell off the raft, then ... well then, that was it.

If not, Derek might still be all right.

布萊恩在激流下游的淺灘上醒來，而木筏早已不知載著德瑞克去哪兒了。布萊恩得克服慌張的情緒，得想像德瑞克還活著，得盡最大的努力去追上木筏……

20

約莫隔天早上的某個什麼時候吧，管它哪一天，一千天、一萬天，他都分不清了。就在那個早上，河幅加寬，往左側轉了個大彎，約有半哩寬。他看見了，或者他認為看見了一座屋頂，樹木間一條看來不自然的直線。

——《領帶河》，p177

Sometime in the morning of the next day, any day, a thousand days or eight days —— he could not tell —— somewhere in that morning the river widened and made a sweeping curve to the left, widened to half a mile or more, and he saw or thought he could see a building roof, a straight line in the trees that did not look natural.

布萊恩不但找回德瑞克，而且經過多天的辛勞，終點，好像就在不遠處⋯⋯

你和朋友的關係是？……

第23頁的小測驗，可以知道你對好友的付出程度，與你們的友誼指數。看看你是哪一種類型吧！

選 **A** 的你：量力而為型　　　　　　　　　　　　　友誼指數 78%

朋友落難，你會衡量現實的情況，再決定究竟要不要兩肋插刀。有時候你的理智會被當成冷漠，但事實往往證明你才是對的。只可惜多數人都是情緒的動物，你可能要做好遭人誤解的心理準備。

選 **B** 的你：自私自利型　　　　　　　　　　　　　友誼指數 63%

朋友有求於你，你不伸出援手也就算了，眼看情況不對，你甚至還會落井下石，真是太恐怖了。當你的朋友，可得小心被你從後面捅一刀啊！

選 **C** 的你：勉強配合型　　　　　　　　　　　　　友誼指數 92%

你好像有很多朋友，但你卻很不快樂，因為你總是壓抑、勉強自己來配合身邊的人。因此，雖然好像每個人都很喜歡你，但對你來說，卻不見得是什麼好事，這樣的友誼，也不是最真實的。

選 **D** 的你：情感優先型　　　　　　　　　　　　　友誼指數 60%

你很容易受到朋友的遭遇或情緒牽動，跟著悲傷、喜悅或憤怒。雖然這是一種貼心的表現，但有時候還是要給對方更具體的幫助或建議，才能讓友誼更上一層樓哦！

划出領帶河，讓我們翻到第40頁，一起去度過寒冬吧！

手斧男孩 3

另一種結局
Brian's Winter

Brian's Winter

- ★歷險指數
- ★關 鍵 字　零下30度、冰天雪地、狩獵
- ★挑戰關卡　禦寒！存糧！手刃大麋鹿！
- ★伴讀利器　兔毛背心、麋鹿皮外套、臭鼬寵物
- ★閱前警語　怕冷的人、缺乏勇氣手刃獵物的人，切勿過冬！
- ★閱讀建議　穿上最保暖的衣物，窩在溫暖的角落！

應變指數測驗 你的臨場反應如何？

在野外露營的你，突然遇到一隻臭鼬朝你擺出攻擊姿勢。

你會：

A.先下手為強，放個屁把臭鼬熏昏　　B.大驚失色，掩面奔逃

C.丟食物試著賄賂臭鼬　　D.無所謂，剛好可以觀察臭鼬的屁股

想知道解答？先跟著布萊恩一起度過嚴苛的寒冬吧！

Brian's Winter

01

那些食物讓他軟弱，讓他想要更多，而且他覺得自己在精神上遠離了森林，遠離了當下。他又恢復成城市小孩，想著漢堡和麥芽奶昔，甚至連做的夢也改變了。

—— 《另一種結局》，p12

It(food) had softened him, made him want more and more, and he could tell that he was moving mentally away from the woods, his situation. He started to think in terms of the city again, of hamburgers and malts, and his dreams changed.

 布萊恩從小飛機中找出救生包，雖然謹慎分配著裡面的食物，可是方便入口的都市食物還是三兩下就吃光光了。

02

這天，有著相同的空氣、相同的太陽、相同的早晨，卻有哪裡不一樣；一股新的涼意、新的觸覺、彷彿臉頰上一個輕柔的吻。

—— 《另一種結局》，p14、15

A new coolness, a touch, a soft kiss on his cheek. It was the same air, the same sun, the same morning, but it was different.

 重新展開狩獵的布萊恩，在提高專注力的同時也慢慢察覺出氣候的變化了。

03

但是，布萊恩變成大自然的一部分，變成了掠奪者，變成長著兩隻腳的狼。有個自然界的基本事實，也幾乎是個定律：為了一隻狼的存活，某些生物必須死去。 ——《另一種結局》，p18

Brian had become part of nature, had become a predator, a two-legged wolf. And there was a physics to it, a basic fact, almost a law: For a wolf to live, something else had to die.

狩獵本領越發純熟的布萊恩，雖然技術卓越，卻不把獵殺當樂趣，因為他深知生物都有求生的本能，只是他的本能讓他不得不獵殺。

04

布萊恩以為每件事都能這樣比照辦理，就像處於某個虛構的、政治正確的社會一樣。不幸的是，熊並不做如是想，使布萊恩深受這個誤解所苦。

—— 《另一種結局》，p29

Unfortunately, the bears did not know that it was an agreement, and Brian was suffering under the misunderstanding that, as in some imaginary politically correct society, everything was working out.

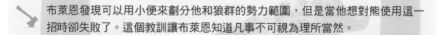

布萊恩發現可以用小便來劃分他和狼群的勢力範圍，但是當他想對熊使用這一招時卻失敗了。這個教訓讓布萊恩知道凡事不可視為理所當然。

05

事實上，熊並不是他的頭號敵人，狼也不是，任何動物都不是。布萊恩變成自己最大的敵人，因為他在打獵、釣魚及求生時，忘了那個最重要的原則：「隨時！隨時都要注意發生了什麼事。」

——《另一種結局》，p33

The bear was not his primary adversary. Nor was the wolf, nor any animal. Brian had become his own worst enemy because in all the business of hunting, fishing and surviving he had forgotten the primary rule: Always, always pay attention to what was happening.

甫遭熊襲擊的布萊恩一面籌思如何在熊出現時保護自己，但與此同時，他似乎還沒有意識到比熊、狼更恐怖的威脅是什麼。

06

問題是他無法確定冬天會有多冷？會下多少雪？或他能做些什麼來生存下去。冬天能夠獵到什麼？　　　　　　——《另一種結局》，p38

The problem... was that he didn't honestly know how cold it would get or how much snow there would be or what he could do to live. What would be available to hunt in the winter?

首次意識到自己必須在此過冬的布萊恩，開始面臨自己對冬天的大自然一無所知的嚴酷挑戰。

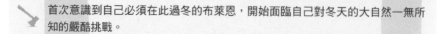

07

那一瞬間，魔力兩個字浮現在他的腦海：「這真是我的魔力箭。」不經思索，這個詞就這樣自然而然地出現了，而他認為這是對的。這不算是什麼信仰，而是一種讓他相信自己曾經做了什麼，以及如何完成的方法。

——《另一種結局》，p46

In the same instant the word medicine came into his thought—It is my medicine arrow. He had not planned it , not meant to think the phrase, but it came and he knew it was right. It was not a religious idea so much as a way to believe in what he had done, and how he had done it, ...

一隻箭射中兩隻獵物，向來辛苦狩獵的布萊恩對於這樣奇妙的成就，下了一個魔力的註腳。

08

那是一個提醒：「光是坐著，什麼事都做不了。」

——《另一種結局》，p53

It was a reminder —— it did not get things done, sitting...

候鳥南遷，寒冬將至的警訊，逼布萊恩展開行動。

09

臭鼬離他不到四呎，窺伺地看著他、棚屋，以及營火。而當布萊恩注意到時，牠突然移動臀部，翻開尾巴，直接瞄準他的臉。

──《另一種結局》，p74

The skunk wasn't four feet away, looking in at him at the shelter and the fire and as he watched, it whipped up its rear end and tipped its tail over and aimed directly at his face.

> 吃過臭鼬虧的布萊恩再次遇上臭鼬，也一樣毫無防備。不過老天眷顧，這一次布萊恩不但沒有被噴，還靠著食物收服了一隻小寵物，並給她取名為貝蒂。

10

但現在有股新的氣味蓋過了熊味，很臭，又像腐味、又像硫磺，令人作嘔的味道。熊一轉身，臭鼬直接將氣味噴在牠眼睛上，賞了個紮紮實實。

──《另一種結局》，p87

Now a new smell, over the smell of the bear; a rank, foul, sulfurous and gagging smell as the bear turned and took a full shot of skunk spray directly in the eyes.

> 貝蒂報恩的機會很快就出現了。有熊來搶布萊恩的鹿肉，偏偏搶肉的動可能會傷害到布萊恩。千鈞一髮之際，貝蒂放出毒氣，擊退這隻熊，也救了布萊恩一命。

11

「會死，」他思索著，這個事實像蛇一般滑入他的腦中。

—— 《另一種結局》，p95

To death, he thought, the truth sliding in like a snake.

 單薄的衣服，連日的冬雨，讓布萊恩明白冬日酷寒將帶來死亡威脅。

12

早上一醒來，他立刻知道有什麼不一樣了，有些聲音變了。不，是不見了，一點聲音也沒有。

—— 《另一種結局》，p97

In the morning he awakened and knew instantly that something had changed. Something about the sound. No. The lack of it.

大地萬物寂靜無聲，宣告冬日初雪降臨。

13

雪是在夜晚降下來，鬆軟的、大量的雪，蓋滿每一個角落，無論是枝幹、樹林、地上，或湖上的冰——所有的地方，統統覆蓋了將近四吋深的雪。 ——《另一種結局》，p98

Snow had fallen in the night. Soft, large flakes, nearly four inches deep everywhere. On limbs, logs, the ground, on the lake ice —— all over, an even four inches.

森林的寒冬初雪，在夜裡悄悄降臨，卻瞬間覆滿大地。

14

家裡的照片已經褪色了，如果他能展示這裡的景象給媽媽看的話，他心裡想，只是想讓她看到這些…… ——《另一種結局》，p101、102

Pictures of home were fading. But if he could show this to his mother, he thought, just for here to see this...

自然美景，令布萊恩忍不住想著怎麼留存這畫面，怎麼與人分享，即便分享這件事，已經離這個遺世獨居的少年非常遙遠了。

15

「好的一天——不，」他想，他的頭腦快停止運作了：「是超棒的一天，一個充滿了肉的日子，一個麋鹿日。」他明天要畫在棚屋的牆上……

——《另一種結局》，p118

A good —— no, he thought, his Brian closing down, a great day. A meat day. A moose day. He would sketch it on the shelter wall tomorrow...

這天是布萊恩的幸運日。見識到森林初雪的美景，又獵得麋鹿一隻獲得豐富食糧，布萊恩忍不住想歌頌這美好的一天……

16

手斧，是所有事物的關鍵。做任何事都少不了它，光是這點就足以
得到他所有的感謝。 ——《另一種結局》，p133

The hatchet. The key to it all. Nothing without the hatchet. Just
that would take all his thanks.

布萊恩在雪中享受著麋鹿肉，他滿懷感謝，最感謝自己的手斧。如果沒有這把
手斧，也許他一開始就輕易放棄自救的希望了……

17

這次打獵相當完美，但這樣的完美也讓布萊恩感到非常不舒服。那
隻鹿在進食，只是在吃東西，而且不知道他在那裡，然後箭就射過
去了…… ——《另一種結局》，p160

In hunting terms it was a perfect kill, and it made Brian feel
perfectly awful. The deer had been eating, just eating, and hadn't
known he was there and the arrow had taken it ...

有了雪鞋，再次活動自如的布萊恩，成功的獵到了一隻鹿，但這結果卻無法讓
他由衷感到高興。畢竟為了求生的他，殺了同樣是為了求生而冒著寒冷出來覓
食的鹿，讓他幾乎覺得自己是謀殺犯。

18

到了晚上，他坐在棚屋的火堆旁，想著這一切怎麼會如此讓人毛骨悚然——自然界怎麼會讓麋鹿遭遇到這種痛苦。

——《另一種結局》，p170

That night in the shelter he sat by fire and wondered how it could be so horrible —— how nature could let an animal suffer the way the moose had suffered.

布萊恩親眼目睹狼群獵殺麋鹿的實況，覺得毛骨悚然，但是也體認到，為了活下去，求取食物的手段是不能計較的。

19

「等你回來時，所有東西都還在這裡，我們會讓湯一直熱著……」

——《另一種結局》，p185

"It will be here when you come back. We'll keep the soup hot ..."

布萊恩終於遇見一戶印第安人。男主人大維體貼不捨離開森林的布萊恩，好好地安慰了他。這是同樣曾經身為森林一分子的人才能理解的感受。

愈緊張，愈慌張？……

第41頁的小測驗，可以知道你在碰上緊急狀況時的反應。看看你是哪一種類型吧！

選**A**的你：搶快型   應變指數 78%
你總是還沒聽清楚問題就急著回答，反應雖然快，但是往往不切實際，甚至牛頭不對馬嘴。縱然奪得先機，沒有好好把握，也是沒有用的。

選**B**的你：棄權型   應變指數 25%
凡事將「棄」、「逃」奉為優先選擇的你，看似明哲保身，實際上根本連狀況都弄不清楚，搞不好會釀出更大的災禍哩！

選**C**的你：謀略型   應變指數 88%
即使情況緊急，你還是能在最短的時間內評估周遭的情勢，想出最適切的方法來因應，讓自己能夠掌握狀況。

選**D**的你：旁觀型   應變指數 68%
你看起來很冷靜，其實是對周遭的一切都不太關心。即使知道該怎麼回應，卻反而會選擇保留或沉默，雖然有時會有意外的收穫，但有時還是會吃虧。

冬天結束後，讓我們翻回到第22頁，順遊領帶河吧！

手斧男孩⁴

Brian's Return

鹿精靈

Brian's Return

★歷險指數　↘↘↘
★關 鍵 字　心理諮商、湖泊、獨木舟、莎士比亞
★挑戰關卡　與熊交鋒、與狼二重唱、化身野獸
★伴讀利器　膽大心細、經典劇本
★閱前警語　站穩腳步，以免被大水沖走！
★閱讀建議　千萬、千萬不要覺得自己已經很行了！

欲望指數測驗　你什麼都想要嗎？

你在森林享受自然生活，也練就一手好箭法。某天你遇上一頭麋鹿，雖然你並不缺乏糧食，但你現在跟牠的距離保證手到擒來。
你會：

A.殺了牠，剛好可以當做練習　　　B.饒了牠，處理起來太麻煩了

C.殺了牠，食物愈多愈好　　　　　D.饒了牠，要吃再獵就好了

想知道解答？先找到屬於你的精靈吧！

Brian's Return

01

隼鷹出獵不是為了屠殺，而是為了覓食。當然，牠得先殺戮才有食物，所有的肉食動物都是如此。但殺戮是獲得食物的手段，不是目的。只有人類會為了運動，或為了戰利品而打獵。

—— 《鹿精靈》，p10

The hawk did not hunt to kill. It hunted to eat. Of course it had to kill to eat —— along with all other carnivorous animals —— but the killing was the means to bring food, not the end. Only man hunted for sport, or for trophies.

> 布萊恩靜靜地坐著，任由獨木舟在睡蓮間漂蕩。過去兩年，他都處於孤獨的痛苦，終於又重新踏回了自然。此刻他順流來到一處小湖泊，背後傳來了隼鷹的嘯聲，布萊恩試著去猜想隼鷹出獵的理由⋯⋯

02

「謀事在人，成事在天」，是他學到的最大重點，偏偏這是人們最難理解，更難以信服的。他根本不是征服了大自然，而是融入其中；大自然成了他的一部分，也許還成了他的全部。

—— 《鹿精靈》，p12

He had learned the most important fact of all, and the one that is so hard for many to understand or believe: Man proposes, nature disposes. he didn't conquered nature at all —— he had become part of it. And it had become part of him, maybe all of him.

> 布萊恩在荒野倖存的經歷讓他小有名氣，報紙、雜誌、電視都來採訪、大肆報導「小男孩征服荒野！」但事情並不是那樣的⋯⋯

03

現實開始打他身旁溜過。並不是他心理上有什麼不正常或病變，而是現實的一切讓他覺得索然無味。 ——《鹿精靈》，p15、16

Reality began to slip away from him. Not that he was mentally different, or mentally ill, so much as that it just bored him.

從荒野裡回到學校之後，布萊恩盡量表現得一如往常，但和他所經歷過的生活相比，一切都顯得黯淡無力。布萊恩身在眾人之中，內心仍是孤獨的。

04

布萊恩簡短地思考了一下，打算告訴她真相：那不是她認識的布萊恩，而是另一個徹頭徹尾不同的人；而且那不是打架，而是自然而然的反射動作。他沒有打架，因為那不是他，那是一頭野獸，一頭男孩般的野獸。不，是看起來像一頭野獸的男孩。

—— 《鹿精靈》，p25

He thought briefly of trying to tell her the truth: that it hadn't been the Brian she knew but a different one, a totally different person; that it hadn't been a fight but an automatic reaction. It hadn't happened because it hadn't been him —— it had been some kind of animal. A boy animal. No, an animal-boy.

 布萊恩意外遭到學校裡另一個男孩的粗暴攻擊，激起了布萊恩在森林中被激發的強悍求生本能。下場是布萊恩必須去看心理醫生。

05

夢裡頭，他已經把一切都打點妥當了。總是這樣，打點妥當，準備要回去，準備要回……回家。回家，到森林去尋找……他不知道要找什麼──尋找他自己，他自己的種種。　　　──《鹿精靈》，p51

It was a dream of getting ready. Always that ── getting ready. Ready to go back. Ready to go ... home. To go home to the woods and find ... he didn't know what. To find himself, something about himself.

整個學校都知道布萊恩的那場打鬥，上學對他而言變成一種煎熬。幾個月後他覺得自己快瘋掉了，只有見到心理醫師卡列伯、以及做那些夢的時候才正常……

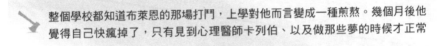

06

他不確定是為什麼。當他四處走動，在屋子裡、穿過市鎮、走在學校裡的時候，他的腦海中根本沒有要回來的念頭。

不論好壞，布萊恩規畫好了他自己的道路。

——《鹿精靈》，p65、66

He wasn't sure why. When he walked around the house or through town or was at school there was not a thought in his mind of coming back.

For better or worse, he was set on his own path.

布萊恩決定去找在冬天曾救過他一命的克里族人斯彭全家，以此作為回去森林的理由。他在打包行李時，發現自己沒有要回來的念頭……

07

布萊恩什麼也沒有說，因為也沒什麼好說的。她是他媽媽，他愛她。他也愛他爸爸，但是他必須這麼做，不然他就會⋯⋯他不知道他會怎麼樣。也許會發瘋，再也無法復原。他內在的某些事物將會死去。

—— 《鹿精靈》，p68

He didn't say anything because there was nothing to say. She was his mother and he loved her. He loved his father too but he had to do this thing or he would ... he didn't know what he would do. Go crazy. Never be right. Somehow inside he would die.

> 布萊恩的母親在送布萊恩上飛機時哭得肝腸寸斷，可是布萊恩知道，他一定得這麼做才行⋯⋯

08

樹葉搖曳、微風吹起、小鳥鳴啼。他緩緩地、靜靜地呼吸，沿著湖岸，和緩地搖動船槳。他將一切盡收眼底，就和過去一樣，完全融入森林。

—— 《鹿精靈》，p103

A leaf that moved, a small bit of wind, the cry of a small bird —— he breathed slowly, quietly, and paddled the canoe gently along the shore. He saw and heard it all, was as absolutely tuned to the woods as he'd ever been.

> 終於到了。布萊恩在蓮葉間划著獨木舟，不慌不忙，從容地享受自己期待已久、時而念及的森林歲月，他想起以前看過的一匹狼，也是那麼的從容⋯⋯

09

他忘了在荒野生活最重要的事情：要提防意外狀況。他原本以為自己永遠不會忘記的。你以為不會碰上，但偏偏就會逮住你。要做最壞的打算，等到真的沒有發生，再來慶幸。

—— 《鹿精靈》，p128

He had forgotten the most important thing about living in the wilderness, the one thing he'd thought he would never forget —— expect the unexpected. What you didn't think would get you, would get you. Plan on the worst and be happy when it didn't come.

布萊恩被初返自然的喜悅沖昏了頭，完全沒去提防意外，風雨交加的一個夜晚，雨水從帳棚下滲入弄濕睡袋，風愈吹愈烈，把帳棚吹塌、獨木舟吹翻……

10

其實，不論他認為事情會怎麼發展，大自然仍然按照自己的規則在進行。布萊恩必須融入其中，深入大自然的本質，而不是他或其他人所揣摩的大自然。

　　　　　　　　　　　　　　　　　　──《鹿精靈》，p132

And finally, no matter what he thought would happen, nature would do what it wanted to do. He had to be part of it, part of what it was really like, not what he or some other person thought it should be like.

前一晚的風雨最糟糕的事情是，布萊恩被散落的箭刺進大腿……這道傷口警惕了他恢復該有的謙卑之心。

11

等他閉上眼睛，睡意逐漸來襲之時，他覺得自己好像看到了那匹狼，或者說，好像看到融入夜色中的牠，穿梭在黑暗裡；樹林的氣味、聲音，猶如水流飛竄過牠身旁；牠駐足傾聽，然後又起步，悄無聲息地溜過月色與森林。

布萊恩與狼已經融為一體，狼就是布萊恩，布萊恩就是狼。

——《鹿精靈》，p140

When he closed his eyes and sleep started to come he thought he could see the wolf, or perhaps see as the wolf moving through the night, part of the night, the smells and sounds of the woods moving through the wolf like vapor, stopping to listen, moving on in a silent slide through the moonlight and forest, Brian and the wolf mixed, Brian-wolf, wolf-Brian.

夜裡，一匹狼在湖泊的彼岸長嚎，布萊恩回應了牠、應和著狼的嚎叫，之後才又鑽回睡袋，他一開始並未入睡，而是回想月光下的那匹狼……

12

這一箭實在太輕鬆了，鐵定十拿九穩。你跑不掉了。布萊恩心想，一股興奮感幾乎就要從咽喉溢出。就要到手了。箭在弦上，布萊恩舉起弓，拉開弦，眼睛一瞄，用寬箭頭瞄準那頭鹿的心臟。最後，他卻停了下來，放鬆弦，垂下了弓。

不要抓鹿，現在還不要，太可惜了。　　　　——《鹿精靈》，p145、146

It would been an easy shot. A clean shot. You're mine, Brian thought, and his throat seemed to choke with it, the excitement. Mine. The arrow was in the bow, he raised the bow, drew the arrow, sighted it so he was looking over the broadhead straight at the deer's heart, and then he paused again. He eased the string up and lowered the bow.

Not the deer, not now. It would be a waste.

布萊恩對著即將到手的獵物，突然放下弓箭，想到炎熱的天氣，鹿肉無法保存只會浪費。他感謝這頭鹿，然後，目送牠離去……

13

這才是我，布萊恩心想：一個獵人。他不再急切，比起殺戮的渴望，他更想看盡眼前一切事物。

——《鹿精靈》，p149

This, he thought, is what I have become. A hunter. The need to hurry disappeared, the need to kill was not as important as the need to see all there was to see.

布萊恩決定今晚在此紮營，要去獵隻松雞或兔子來飽餐一頓。但是他不想要急切地狩獵，他要看盡、感受這一切。

14

「我今天看到一頭鹿,就在我前面。牠停下來看著我,掉過頭去,又回過頭來。我原本可以射牠的……」布萊恩不知道自己為什麼要說這些,但似乎該將這件事說出來。

「牠掉過頭去,是不是在看你要去的方向?」

布萊恩想了想:「沒錯。朝北順著陸運道。」

比利點點頭:「那是你的鹿精靈,牠在告訴你正確的方向。」

—— 《鹿精靈》,p156、157

"I saw a deer today, walking here. It stood and looked at me, then away, then back. I could have shot it ..." Brian didn't know why he said this, only that it seemed the right thing to do.

"Did it look the way you are going when it looked away?"

Brian thought about it. "Yes. North, up the portage."

Billy nodded. "It was your medicine deer, telling you the right way to go."

打獵回到營地的布萊恩,發現一個外表歷經風霜的男人正在生火。這位偶然相逢的陌生客 —— 比利,讓布萊恩起了莫名的好感,他們兩人吃完晚餐後,坐在火堆旁聊了起來……

15

我今天才明白，只要你準備好了，其實不需要真的動手。

整理獨木舟的時候，布萊恩覺得自己躍躍欲試，準備朝著地平線和天際尋回自己。不是去思考自己或衡量自我價值，只是一邊走，一邊好好看著這個世界。

——《鹿精靈》，p159、160

I found today that you don't always have to do a thing as long as you're ready to do it.

Brian felt himself looking out as he packed the canoe, looking out of himself ahead at the horizon, the sky; not thinking of himself or what he was about but just seeing the world as he moved through it.

隔天布萊恩神清氣爽的醒來，比利早就走了，但比利把他自己的精靈和鹿精靈的象徵留給布萊恩——一隻烏鴉羽毛和一撮鹿的尾巴，布萊恩想著比利教他的事情，要好好地看這世界……

16

現在布萊恩沒什麼好準備了。箭和弓弦在他的指間微微顫動，寬箭頭對準了熊的心窩，那頭熊就站在那兒看著布萊恩。鳥也不唱歌了，獨木舟旁的漣漪也靜止了，這個世界只剩一個人和一頭熊，其他什麼都沒有。這一刻比時間更加蒼老，一個人、一頭熊、一片死寂。

—— 《鹿精靈》，p165

There was nothing else for Brian then but the arrow and the bowstring trembling slightly in his fingers and the broadhead that he would send into the bear's heart and the bear standing there, looking at him —— no birds singing, no ripple of water past the canoe, no other thing in the world but one man and one bear in a moment perhaps older than time, a bear, a man and quiet death.

布萊恩沿著溪流涉水時，遇到了熊。這隻年輕的熊盯上了他、打算玩弄他，布萊恩一路後退、衝到獨木舟旁抄起了弓、上箭對準了熊。弓弦繃緊了，只要熊一靠近，布萊恩就會放箭⋯⋯

17

他知道自己沒有恐懼，因為他和熊同樣有本事、同樣矯健、同樣為該做的事蓄勢待發。

——《鹿精靈》，p167

He was not afraid because he was as good as the bear, as quick, as ready to do what he had to do.

> 熊離去了，沒有回頭。布萊恩放鬆了下來，感受自己的心靈到了屬於自己的地方：他與熊、與自然、與生命，都是均衡的。

18

地圖很大。有許多湖泊、河流可以見識，更有大片的田園可以徜徉其中。他還要再往前走一會兒，也許隨著日落往西方去。

——《鹿精靈》，p171

It was a big map. There were many lakes and rivers to see, much more country to be in. He would head this way for a time, then perhaps move west with the sun.

> 布萊恩做了個夢，夢見比利是他的精靈。布萊恩隻身出發，卻不在往斯彭家的路上，斯彭家晚點再說吧，時候到了就會遇上，他打算再往前走、走向他的人生。

是想要，還是需要？……

第57頁的小測驗，可以知道你對物質的渴望程度。看看你是哪種類型吧！

選**A**的你：純粹享樂型　　　　　　　　欲望指數 98%

「只要想，就要得到！」這句話幾乎是你人生的座右銘。不論何時，只要是能感到快樂，任何事情你都會去做，一切都以滿足自我為優先。

選**B**的你：安逸懶散型　　　　　　　　欲望指數 19%

能夠阻止你的欲望者，只有一個「懶」字。你會因為懶而選擇不要什麼、不做什麼，只要坐著就能完成的事情，你絕對不會站起來做。懶到最高點，心中無欲望。

選**C**的你：未雨綢繆型　　　　　　　　欲望指數 84%

崇尚「有備無患，再備平安」的你，是那種會在打折季節購買一堆東西來囤積的人。雖然好像有點貪心，其實只是想要從中多獲得一點安全感而已。

選**D**的你：知足常樂型　　　　　　　　欲望指數 66%

覺得「夠用就好」的你，面對一項物品，即使再怎麼想要，也會以「是否需要」為優先考量。自制力極佳，也很少會有浪費的情形發生。

找到屬於你的精靈了嗎？整理好你的裝備，往下一頁蓄勢待發吧！

手斧男孩5
Brian's Hunt
獵殺布萊恩

Brian's Hunt

★歷險指數　↘↘↘↘↘
★關 鍵 字　狗、熊、陷阱、狩獵
★挑戰關卡　線索、智慧、小心翼翼！
★伴讀利器　弓、箭、靈敏的四肢與五官
★閱前警語　膽小者、粗心者，盡快閃人！
★閱讀建議　打開所有知覺，屏氣凝神！

Brian's Hunt

01

能夠隨心所欲地生火，是多麼美好的事；每當他坐下來煮飯時，都會笑著想起他的荒野生涯是如何展開的。那次孤獨的初體驗。

——《獵殺布萊恩》，p8

He still could not get over how wonderful it was to just be able to make a fire when he wanted one, and he never sat down to a cook fire without smiling and remembering when his life in the wilderness had begun. His first time alone.

> 布萊恩回家了；回到荒野中。這次他有獨木舟和弓箭、乾糧、茶葉、簡單的炊具，甚至還帶了火柴。他生火時，都會想到以前的事情，但像墜機這樣的惡夢愈來愈少，現在他回想起的，都是第一個月獨自在森林中愉快的回憶……

02

初到森林時，他挨餓挨了很久……食物是天大地大的事，只要一想到會浪費任何食物，他就感到全身不對勁。

——《獵殺布萊恩》，p13

He had gone hungry so long when he had first come to the bush ... Food had been everything and the thought of wasting any of it went against every instinct in his body.

> 即使布萊恩有了強大的武器，仍不允許自己浪費食物，他只會獵殺足以吃完的分量，因此他也不會輕易對鹿或麋鹿下手，那分量太多了。

03

他心中記掛著要去看看山林景致，往北就是了。南方都是都市與人潮。他很快就覺得人類這種生物過日子、對待地球的方式都是不好的，大多數情況下，甚至是醜陋且錯誤的。

—— 《獵殺布萊恩》，p16

He had in mind to go see that country. Just head north. South was cities, people, and he was fast coming to think that people, and what people did with their lives, with their world, were not good, were in most cases ugly and wrong.

布萊恩依舊往北走，要去見斯彭家 —— 曾經在雪地裡救他的一家人。但他同樣掛念的是北方的自然，而非滿是人潮的南方，人的作為，讓他無法忍受。

04

他回到自己的天地，回到荒野之中。他曾經回到文明世界，但發誓再也不要回去了。但他並不想離開學校，因為他發現有件不可思議的事情可以伴隨學習而來：你學到東西了。

—— 《獵殺布萊恩》，p19

He had returned to his world, the wilderness. He had sworn that he wouldn't, once he'd gone back to civilization. But he didn't want to do that because he had discovered that there was this incredible thing that happened with studying: you learned things.

雖然他無法忍受文明世界，但他熱愛學習。在森林之中每個決斷都攸關生死，他得試圖瞭解所遇到的一切狀況。這使得他回到學校之後，對知識有強烈的渴望，他試著對眼前所有事物都深入探究。

05

因為他無法在文明世界與他人相處，他知道自己或許永遠無法適應，於是現在的他回到森林裡。但他並不討厭學校，或是讀書學習的念頭。

——《獵殺布萊恩》，p22

And though he had come back to the bush now because he couldn't be with the people back in civilization, and because he knew he would probably never fit in, he did not hate school, or the concept of studying and learning.

➤ 因為他真正的在學習了，所以他並不討厭讀書的念頭，可是他無法與截然不同的人共處，他得找出自己與這個世界的平衡。

06

他現在的行動，也就是狩獵方式，好像是在進行一場追蹤。很久以前他就學到欲速則不達的道理，不管要獵什麼，從魚到糜鹿，最重要的關鍵所在，絕對就是耐心。你得花掉該花的時間。

——《獵殺布萊恩》，p27

Just like so much of what he did now, so much of how he hunted, it was a stalking procedure. He had learned long ago that to hurry is to lose. Patience was the key, the absolutely most important part of hunting anything, from fish to moose. You needed to take the time required.

➤ 布萊恩從往事中回到現實，他放棄獵殺那隻鹿，但他仍須找食物餵飽自己。而蓮葉底下躺著一隻狗魚，狗魚身手矯捷、警覺性高，布萊恩可是需要極大的耐心才能獵捕牠們，而他在狩獵中學會最重要的事就是耐心。

07

他把眼前的肉塊當作是一頓不會走路的大餐，是一頓長眠不醒的佳餚。

——《獵殺布萊恩》，p31

What he had come to think of as a can't-walk-meal, or a lie-down-and-sleep-meal.

> 布萊恩小心翼翼的划槳，又在獨木舟上匍匐向前抽出箭來……他無懈可擊地射中了那尾狗魚。而布萊恩在狩獵成功之後，總是會感謝他的獵物賜給他這一餐。

08

布萊恩變了。起初他以為是自己做事的方法有好幾個階段，而他又進入了下一個階段。但他意識到，自己已隨著周遭環境的變遷，隨著見識愈來愈廣，不斷在改變著。　　——《獵殺布萊恩》，p35

He had changed. He thought at first that he had changed again, that there were steps in how he had done so, but he realized that he was changing constantly as the world around him shifted, as he learned more.

> 布萊恩隨著環境的改變、和自己見識的增長而不斷在調整適應著。就像紮營這件事，他已經不需要像飛機失事那時，找個地方安頓下來，現在他盡快找塊空地、停好獨木舟、熟練的釣魚生火。這種自由和行動力使得他可以一邊狩獵、一邊向目的地移動。

但他現在知道，只要有古怪的狀況，即使是一點不尋常的蛛絲馬跡、不尋常的聲響、奇怪的顏色或氣味，就要有所反應。

而此時此地，所有奇特的聲響、色彩、氣味、蛛絲馬跡都有其意義。

——《獵殺布萊恩》，p43、44

But so much of him was tuned now to reacting to odd things, a line that did not belong where it was, a sound that should not be there, an odd color or smell.

Here, now, every odd sound or color or line or smell meant something.

布萊恩睡得很熟，而且正在做夢，可是他被聲音驚醒了⋯⋯在自然裡，所有不尋常的聲音和細節，都有其意義。

10

這一切太詭異了。在森林中，有任何不尋常的事情都要仔細琢磨。這兒有隻狗，把布萊恩當朋友般歡迎，為什麼呢？為什麼有隻狗？為什麼在這裡？會不會不只如此，還有別人在？是不是有什麼在岸邊等著布萊恩，可能會會對他不利？ —— 《獵殺布萊恩》，p51

This was all very strange, and strange things in the bush often deserved more study. The dog was here, she greeted Brian as a friend, but why? Why a dog? Why was it here? Was there more to it, more people here, something possibly not good waiting for him on the bank?

一隻狗在岸邊哀鳴，是條母狗，人們常常養在營地裡的阿拉斯加拖橇犬，可是牠不但離開主人，而且半邊身體鮮血淋淋，怎麼一回事？

11

附近沒有人。

然而，有一隻狗在這裡。這隻狗顯然是有人豢養的，希望和人類作伴，而且牠看來削瘦，沒辦法自給自足地狩獵。牠需要和人類在一起，卻不知為何和人走散了。

—— 《獵殺布萊恩》，p61

Nobody was close.

And yet, here was the dog. Obviously a person dog, a dog that wanted to be with humans, a dog that couldn't hunt for herself well —— she looked thin —— and needed to be with people yet had, for some reason, left her people?

> 布萊恩的本能和直覺已經接近森林裡的動物了，他感覺得出來附近沒有人。然而這隻狗顯然是人所養的，為什麼會走散而不是回家，卻又負傷這麼嚴重？

12

他現在有朋友了，是個新朋友。他微笑著想到，這是第一隻狗，他的第一隻狗。雖然就事實上來說，牠並不是隻寵物；與其說牠屬於布萊恩，倒不如說牠是自己的主宰。

但牠是布萊恩的朋友，落難的朋友。俗話說，患難見真情。

—— 《獵殺布萊恩》，p78

He had a friend now, a new friend, and he smiled, thinking, First dog, his first dog, although technically she wasn't really a pet and truly belonged to herself more than she did to Brian.

But she was a friend, a friend in need, and as the cliche said, a friend in need was a friend indeed.

> 回到營地，就著白天的光線，布萊恩仔細檢查狗兒身上的傷口，有爪子、也不是被咬的，可以篤定是熊了，但為何受攻擊後卻逃離自己的家……不論如何，這是他的新朋友。

13

有一股詭異的氣氛壓在他心頭，盤旋不去。

沒有輪廓、沒有方向，只是一股詭異的不安，好像在某個地方有某件事，是他必須要親眼、親耳、親身去體驗、去完成的……在哪裡呢？

—— 《獵殺布萊恩》，p79

And yet it was there, the odd feeling, the odd feeling, the odd push in his mind.

No plan, no direction, just a strange unease as if there was something he needed to see or do or hear or feel somewhere ... where?

布萊恩感受到迫切感，想要快點採取行動。就零星跡象顯示，狗兒是北方來的，他們該往北方打探，順道看看朋友……只是不安感一直在布萊恩心中。

14

從某種角度來看，這隻狗彌補了他生命中的缺憾，撫慰了他從未意識到的寂寞，他懷疑是不是人類一直以來都是如此。

—— 《獵殺布萊恩》，p95

In some way, the dog filled a hole in his life, filled a loneliness he hadn't even known existed, and he wondered if it had always been the same for men.

才過兩天不到，布萊恩驚訝於他和狗兒如此投契，他端詳著狗兒入睡；狗兒一坐起身，布萊恩也看著牠，觀察牠的反應、依靠牠的警告，好提防事情發生。

15

黎明的第一道曙光乍現，布萊恩卻已經在打包行李準備離開。這會兒，布萊恩憑藉的多半是本能、是感覺，他習慣稱之為直覺。他認為，這是在潛意識中，藉由自己有時也不甚明瞭的知識，結合資訊，一路演繹而成的。
而且，這直覺通常是正確的，布萊恩學會信從它。

—— 《獵殺布萊恩》，p96

Dawn, first light, found him packing the canoe to leave. So much of what drove Brian now was instinct, feelings, what he used to call hunches but what he now thought of as logical flows of information from his subconscious based on knowledge that he sometimes did not quite understand.
Usually, it was right and he had learned to trust it.

布萊恩雖然想要隔天繼續紮營、在火堆邊悠哉地吃肉。但他的直覺驅促他出航，不尋常的急迫感讓他一頭霧水。布萊恩確定狗兒的傷口是熊造成的、但狗兒不會只是被打傷就離開營地……整件事一點也不合邏輯，布萊恩得趕快上路查明。

16

沒有什麼風吹草動。之前一直都有些事情發生，顯示著自然的運作。但來到這裡，情況就不一樣了。這裡有著先前所沒有的安靜，但不是獨木舟經過所致。他沒有看到鳥，更重要的是，連聽都沒聽到。

這兒有人類，他往人類靠近了。　　　　——《獵殺布萊恩》，p101、102

There was less sound, less small movement. Before, there had always been something happening, some indication of nature, and here ... it had changed. A quieting that wasn't there before, and not caused by the canoe passing. He hadn't seen birds, but more, hadn't heard them either.

There was man here; he was getting close to man.

往北划了快一整天，走了三十哩還沒看到營地。隔天也是天一亮就出航，終於，他發現四周起了變化，他向人類靠近了……

17

一股味道撲鼻而來。不是煙味，不是木頭的煙味，而是血腥味。是腐敗的血肉發出濃烈、腐壞的臭味。

他心想，好吧，好吧！他們留了些肉在這裡，有什麼東西闖進小屋裡攫取肉塊，讓蒼蠅飛了進來，然後……然後……然後……。

完全不是這樣，大錯特錯！他這一生中從未感到如此強烈的錯誤，他的身心都渴望著逃跑，渴望離開這個地方。但他知道自己必須前進，走進那間小屋……

—— 《獵殺布萊恩》，p109、110

Then the smell hit him. Not smoke, not woodsmoke, but the smell of blood, musty, rotten smell of spoiled blood and flesh.

All right, he thought. All right. They left some meat here and something broke into the cabin and got at it and let the flies in and ... and ... and ...

It was all wrong. So wrong. He had never felt anything so powerfully wrong in his life and everything in him wanted to run, get away from this place, but he knew he had to go on, to go in the cabin...

島上沒有人，似乎是離開了。營區的小屋門敞開著，狗兒停了下來發出低沉的吼聲。布萊恩搭起弓向小屋靠近，他聞到了一股血腥味……

18

布萊恩無法思考，什麼也做不了，除了在旁嘔吐，試著說服自己剛剛看到的不是真的。不會這樣。不會真的就這麼發生了，不要這樣，不要是這麼可怕的事情……

布萊恩的腦海中有一部分在自動運作，他看到自己目不忍睹的事情，但無法讓自己坦然接受。　　　　——《獵殺布萊恩》，p112、113

He couldn't think, couldn't react, couldn't do anything except stand and throw up and try to make what he had seen not exist. It couldn't be. It just couldn't actually be, not this, not this terrible thing....

A part of Brian's Brain went on automatic and saw things he could not stand to look at, could not bring himself to openly acknowledge.

> 小屋內所有的東西都被撕成碎片散落一地，布萊恩心裡有數，可是他不願意承認，然後，他看到了蒼蠅聚集的角落裡有東西……他的朋友斯彭一家人遭受攻擊慘死。

19

布萊恩從未見過那頭動物，但他對那頭熊瞭若指掌。包括牠走路的方式、轉身的方式、思考的方式。就算那頭熊站在他們面前，他們眼中只有重量、體長、毛色、基因編碼，以及細胞信號，但從不曾真正去認識那頭熊。　　　　　　　　　　——《獵殺布萊恩》，p135

Brian had never seen the animal but knew the bear intimately, how it moved, how it turned, how it thought. They could be looking right at it and all they would see would be weight and girth and hair color and genetic codes and biospeak and would never really know the bear.

> 蘇珊找出無線電呼叫有關單位，很快的，騎警和自然資源管理處的人都來了，但他們不確定要處分哪一頭熊，森林中有太多熊了。布萊恩什麼也沒說，但他明白那些人錯了，他認得出這頭熊，他會找出來。

20

牠很懶散。牠不爬坡，而是從坡邊繞過；翻動圓木、扒開殘幹，牠的爪痕與眾不同。牠的左邊前掌上缺了一隻爪子，右爪有一隻斷了一半。在泥巴或軟土中，很輕易就能看透牠、瞭解牠。

—— 《獵殺布萊恩》，p141

He was lazy. He did not climb hills but worked around the base of them instead, turning logs, ripping stumps, and he had distinctive paw marks. One claw was gone on his left front paw and one broken in half on his right. In mud or soft dirt it was easy to read him, know him.

下定決心要為友復仇的布萊恩，發揮犯罪鑑識的本領，觀察那頭熊留下的各種痕跡，更了解自己的敵人。

21

在那漫長無涯的一剎那，布萊恩從獵人變成了獵物，背脊一陣寒意。鹿被狼群相中的時候，肯定就是這種感覺。狐狸開始追逐的時候，兔子肯定就是這種感覺。寒徹心肺，無法呼吸；時間暫停，無法思考。一剎那間，有某種感受壓過了恐懼，一種非常古老、非常原始的感受。

那頭熊獵殺的對象，就是布萊恩。　　　——《獵殺布萊恩》，p145、146

And for just that second, that long, long second, Brian went from predator to prey, felt a coldness on his neck, felt as a deer must feel when the wolves pick up its scent, as a rabbit must feel when the fox starts its run... cold, no breath, everything stopped. No thinking. Just that long second of something even more than fear, something very old, very primitive.

The bear was hunting him.

布萊恩又走回之前攀越過的一座丘陵，他發現自己在兜圈子，也看到了剛剛走來的路上，留有一塊清晰的腳印，碩大無朋的腳印缺了隻爪子，而且是剛剛才踏上的。是牠⋯⋯

22

那頭熊倒地而死，布萊恩試著仿效那隻狗，尋找一點勝利的感動與獲勝的喜悅。然而，現在他腦海中都是大維和安，還有蘇珊和她的弟妹這一生所要蒙受的巨大傷痛。他認為不只如此，他甚至希望能夠感覺到其他事物。但什麼都沒有，只有失去朋友的感覺。

他殺了一頭熊，不過就是這麼一回事。

——《獵殺布萊恩》，p152

The bear lay dead and Brian tried to find some feeling of triumph, as the dog had, some sense of victory, but all he could think of were David and Anne and the great loss that Susan and her brother and sister had in their lives now. He had thought there would be more. He even hoped that he would feel more. But there was nothing but the loss of his friends.

It was just what it was, a dead bear.

布萊恩只聽到穿林而出的聲音，他還來不及拉弓箭就被一掌打飛。突然狗兒狂吠、跳上熊的背部，熊轉身攻擊、一掌把狗兒揮到二十碼外，這當中有兩秒的空檔，布萊恩從地上散落的箭中抄起一支來，往熊的胸口刺去……

該不該相信第六感？……

第75頁的小測驗，可以知道你的直覺敏感度。看看你是哪一種類型吧！

選A的你：遲鈍無感型　　　　　　　　　　　　　　直覺指數 2%

你的神經大概就像電線桿那麼粗，天大的預兆顯示在你眼前，你也視而不見。神經大條雖然可以省去一些無謂的擔憂，不過有時候也會讓你身陷危險而不自知。

選B的你：妄想過度型　　　　　　　　　　　　　　直覺指數 47%

雖然你偶爾會有一些說不上來的直覺，但你卻很容易渲染、放大它們，甚至憑空捏造，讓自己處在草木皆兵的情境之下。你實在太容易自己嚇自己了。

選C的你：細心敏銳型　　　　　　　　　　　　　　直覺指數 92%

你有著準確的第六感，在這些靈光一閃的時刻，你也能理智地做出適切的判斷，而非一味地全盤接受。這些感覺是你在現實生活中趨吉避凶的好幫手，要好好運用。

選D的你：置之不理型　　　　　　　　　　　　　　直覺指數 72 %

你是個重視「實證」的人。什麼直覺、第六感，縱使真的閃過腦海，你也是鐵齒地不願意理會它。放下那些科學理論，偶爾相信自己腦中的聲音吧！

結束了驚險萬分的英語求生，你是不是也像布萊恩一樣，更瞭解自己了呢？

故事盒子8

作　　者　蓋瑞‧伯森 Gary Paulsen

總 編 輯　張瑩瑩
副總編輯　蔡麗真
責任編輯　李依蒨
校　　對　袁若喬
美術設計　洪素貞 (suzan1009@gmail.com)
封面設計　李東記
行銷企畫　林麗紅

社　　長　郭重興
發行人兼
出版總監　曾大福
出　　版　野人文化股份有限公司
發　　行　遠足文化事業股份有限公司
　　　　　地址：231 新北市新店區民權路 108-2 號 9 樓
　　　　　電話：（02）2218-1417　傳真：（02）8667-1065
　　　　　電子信箱：service@bookrep.com.tw
　　　　　網址：www.bookrep.com.tw
　　　　　郵撥帳號：19504465 遠足文化事業股份有限公司
　　　　　客服專線：0800-221-029
法律顧問　華洋法律事務所 蘇文生律師
印　　製　成陽印刷股份有限公司
初　　版　2006 年 2 月
二　　版　2012 年 7 月
二版16刷　2017 年 7 月

歡迎團體訂購，另有優惠，請洽業務部（02）22181417 分機 1124、1126

國家圖書館出版品預行編目 (CIP) 資料

手斧男孩 . 6, 英語求生 100 天：手斧男孩中英名
句選 / 蓋瑞 . 伯森 (Gary Paulsen) 著 . -- 二版 . --
新北市：野人文化出版：遠足文化發行 , 2012.07
　　面；　公分 . -- (故事盒子；8)
　ISBN 978-986-5947-05-7(平裝)

1. 英語 2. 讀本

805.18　　　　　　　　　　　101008050

野人文化
讀者回函卡

姓　名 ＿＿＿＿＿＿＿＿＿ □女 □男　年齡 ＿＿＿＿＿

地　址 ＿＿＿＿＿＿＿＿＿＿＿＿＿＿＿＿＿＿＿＿＿＿＿

電　話 公 ＿＿＿＿＿＿ 宅 ＿＿＿＿＿ 手機 ＿＿＿＿＿

Email ＿＿＿＿＿＿＿＿＿＿＿＿＿＿＿＿＿＿＿＿＿＿＿＿

學　歷 □國中(含以下) □高中職　　□大專　　　□研究所以上
職　業 □生產/製造 □金融/商業　□傳播/廣告　□軍警/公務員
　　　　□教育/文化 □旅遊/運輸　□醫療/保健　□仲介/服務
　　　　□學生　　　□自由/家管 □其他

◆你從何處知道此書？
　□書店 □書訊 □書評 □報紙 □廣播 □電視 □網路
　□廣告 DM □親友介紹 □其他

◆你以何種方式購買本書？
　□誠品書店 □誠品網路書店 □金石堂書店 □金石堂網路書店
　□博客來網路書店 □其他 ＿＿＿＿＿＿＿＿＿＿＿

◆你的閱讀習慣：
　□百科 □生態 □文學 □藝術 □社會科學 □地理地圖
　□民俗采風 □休閒生活 □圖鑑 □歷史 □建築 □傳記
　□自然科學 □戲劇舞蹈 □宗教哲學 □其他

◆你對本書的評價：(請填代號，1. 非常滿意 2. 滿意 3. 尚可 4. 待改進)
　書名 ＿＿＿ 封面設計 ＿＿＿ 版面編排 ＿＿＿ 印刷 ＿＿＿ 內容 ＿＿＿
　整體評價 ＿＿＿

◆你對本書的建議：

＿＿＿＿＿＿＿＿＿＿＿＿＿＿＿＿＿＿＿＿＿＿＿＿＿＿＿

＿＿＿＿＿＿＿＿＿＿＿＿＿＿＿＿＿＿＿＿＿＿＿＿＿＿＿

＿＿＿＿＿＿＿＿＿＿＿＿＿＿＿＿＿＿＿＿＿＿＿＿＿＿＿

＿＿＿＿＿＿＿＿＿＿＿＿＿＿＿＿＿＿＿＿＿＿＿＿＿＿＿

＿＿＿＿＿＿＿＿＿＿＿＿＿＿＿＿＿＿＿＿＿＿＿＿＿＿＿

廣　告　回　函
板橋郵政管理局登記證
板橋廣字第 143 號

郵資已付　免貼郵票

野人

23141
新北市新店區民權路108-3號6樓
野人文化股份有限公司 收

請沿線撕下對折寄回

野人

書名：**手斧男孩 6 英語求生 100 天**
手斧男孩中英名句選（十萬冊紀念版）

書號：0NSB4008